This book belongs to

Ogidk

Heather Hill

Sundown Hill

Golden Meadow

Crystal Cave

Moonshine Pond

Dewdrop Spring

Honeydew Meadow

Mulberry Bushes

Misty Wood Rabbit Warren

HOME SWEET HOME

How many **Fairy Animals** books have you collected?

 Chloe the Kitten

 Bella the Bunny

 Paddy the Puppy

 Mia the Mouse

And there are lots more magical adventures coming very soon!

Fairy Animals
of Misty Wood

Paddy the Puppy

Lily Small

EGMONT

With special thanks to Gill Harvey

EGMONT

We bring stories to life

Paddy the Puppy first published in Great Britain 2013
by Egmont UK Limited
The Yellow Building, 1 Nicholas Road, London W11 4AN

Text copyright © 2013 Hothouse Fiction Ltd
Illustrations copyright © 2013 Kirsteen Harris Jones
All rights reserved

The moral rights of the illustrator have been asserted

ISBN 978 1 4052 6036 7
1 3 5 7 9 10 8 6 4 2

www.egmont.co.uk

www.hothousefiction.com

www.fairyanimals.com

A CIP catalogue record for this title is available from the British Library

Printed and bound in Great Britain by The CPI Group

50046/4

MIX
Paper
FSC   FSC® C018306

EGMONT LUCKY COIN

Our story began over a century ago, when seventeen-year-old
Egmont Harald Petersen found a coin in the street.

He was on his way to buy a flyswatter, a small hand-operated
printing machine that he then set up in his tiny apartment.

The coin brought him such good luck that today Egmont has
offices in over 30 countries around the world. And that lucky
coin is still kept at the company's head offices in Denmark.

Contents

Chapter One: A Very Exciting Morning   1

Chapter Two: Aaahhh-tchoo!   20

Chapter Three: Happy Birthday to Me!   40

Chapter Four: Where's My Breakfast?   59

Chapter Five: Paddy's Perfect Cushion   78

Chapter Six: The Best Birthday Party Ever   97

CHAPTER ONE

A Very Exciting Morning

The sun had just come out to play
above Misty Wood. Golden light
danced all over the fresh green
leaves of the trees and warmed the

1

beautiful flowers in the valleys and meadows. Everything was bursting with colour.

In a cosy den under the Hawthorn Hedgerows, sparkling sunbeams nudged the mossy bed of Paddy the Pollen Puppy. Paddy was curled up in a furry ball, but he wasn't asleep. He'd been awake for *ages*. Today was his birthday, and he'd woken up early because he was so excited!

Paddy gazed around the den

at his mum, his dad and his sister,

Pippa. Their floppy ears were laid

3

over their front legs, and their eyes were shut tight.

'Uhhh . . . hmmm,' snored Paddy's dad, his fluffy tail twitching.

'Hmmm . . . uhhh,' snored his mum, her silky ears quivering.

Paddy sighed. 'I wish they'd wake up,' he said to himself.

He got up and padded round in a circle on his cushion of moss. Round and round and round.

Soon he felt dizzy, so he flopped down again. He wriggled on to his back and waved his white paws in the air. Then he rolled over and opened his glittery yellow wings. He longed to fly across and pounce on his mum's back, or give his sister's tail a playful tug. But he knew he shouldn't. They would be cross if he woke them up early.

Like all the other fairy animals in Misty Wood, Pollen Puppies had

an important job to do. They had
to flick pollen around the meadows
with their tails so that the flowers
could grow. It was very busy work,
so they needed plenty of sleep.

Paddy decided to think about
his birthday party while he waited
for everyone to wake up.

*It's going to be the best party
EVER*, he thought. *There'll be
hazelnut cake and elderflower pop and
sticky chestnut buns, and we'll collect*

6

bubbles from Moonshine Pond and blow them all over the wood!

His tail began to wag at the very idea.

But, first of all, I'll have to open my presents. Paddy grinned, showing his velvety pink tongue. *I wonder what Mum and Dad have got for me this year . . .*

He looked around the den. His present must be hidden somewhere. His mum, dad and sister were all

sleeping on comfy moss cushions, just like his. Maybe they'd slipped his present underneath one of them? But no – then it would get squashed. It must be somewhere else.

Paddy stretched his wings and hopped off his cushion. He checked the beautiful cobweb that hung above the entrance to the den. It had already been decorated with sparkling dewdrops by the

8

Cobweb Kittens. But apart from the dewdrops, glistening like jewels in the sun, the cobweb was empty. There was still no sign of Paddy's present.

'It must be here *somewhere*,' Paddy muttered.

He put his shiny pink nose in the air and sniffed. But he couldn't smell anything apart from the sweet scent of flowers drifting down from the meadow.

He peered under the four red-and-white toadstools that the family sat on to eat their meals.

Nothing.

He nudged the pile of berries that he and Pippa played catching games with.

Nothing there either.

He peeped into the corner of the den where his dad liked to sit chewing sticks.

No. Not a thing!

Disappointed, Paddy wandered
back over to his cushion. As he
clambered on to it, he looked up.

And there, wedged into the bush
above his mum and dad and
Pippa, was a very strange shape.
Paddy stared at it. He was sure
it hadn't been there before.

His tail started wagging again.

It must be his present!

The mystery shape wasn't too big, and it wasn't too small. It wasn't exactly round, but it wasn't square either. Paddy started panting with excitement, trying to work out what it could be. Maybe it was a soft grassy brush to keep his fur and wings tidy. Or maybe it was a daisy-chain collar to wear on special occasions – like

birthday parties. Or, best of all, maybe it was a bone – a big, fat, juicy bone that he could sit and chew on for weeks!

Paddy was so excited he wanted to jump up and down. He was so excited he wanted to bounce all around. He was so excited he wanted to spread his shimmering wings and buzz about like a Misty Wood bee. He just couldn't lie on his bed

14

a moment longer. Paddy did a forward roll off his cushion and landed near his mum and dad. Maybe if he got a little bit closer to the shape he'd be able to sniff it . . . and then he might be able to guess what it was.

But the shape was hard to reach. It was sitting in the arch of a hawthorn branch that curved right over his mum and dad's bed. If he was going to get any closer

to it, he'd have to climb up the branch, just a little bit . . .

Paddy placed one paw on the bottom of the branch. Then he hooked another paw a little higher.

CREEEEEAAAAK went the branch.

Oh, no! thought Paddy.

But his mum and dad stayed asleep.

Paddy placed one of his front paws even higher still.

CREEEEEAAAAK went the branch.

Oh, no! thought Paddy.

But still his mum and dad stayed asleep.

Breathing a sigh of relief, Paddy climbed even higher. Soon he'd be able to sniff the mysterious shape and work out what it was.

CREEEEEAAAAK went the branch.

Oh, no! thought Paddy.

CRACK went the branch as it gave way.

Oh, no! Oh, no! Oh, no! thought Paddy as his paws slipped. He was so shocked he didn't even have time to flap his wings. Instead, he tumbled down and landed with a bump – right on top of his mum and dad!

CHAPTER TWO

Aaahhh-tchoo!

'Paddy!' his mum and dad cried
as they leaped out of bed, their fur
standing on end.

'Oops!' yelped Paddy. 'Sorry,
Mum! Sorry, Dad!'

Paddy's dad had been so
startled that he'd jumped all the
way on to Pippa's mossy bed.

'Help! The sky's fallen on top
of me!' Pippa cried, waving her
silky paws in the air.

'Don't worry, Pippa,' her mum
said. 'It's only Dad.'

'But why has *Dad* fallen on
top of me?' Pippa asked sleepily.

Paddy's dad scampered back
to his own cushion. 'Because

21

Paddy fell on top of *me*,' he said.
'Whatever were you doing, Paddy?
You've woken us all up!'

Paddy covered his eyes with
his paws. 'I didn't mean to,' he
whimpered. 'I just saw the shape
up in the bush and I thought it
might be . . . might be . . . my . . .'

Paddy had given everyone
such a shock he didn't even dare
mention his birthday. He peeped
between his paws, hoping they

weren't all too upset.

'Ah, of course!' His mum
smiled. 'You thought it was your
present! Happy birthday, Paddy!'

Paddy's dad smoothed
down his brown and cream fur

and patted Paddy's head. 'Don't worry, Paddy. It was time to get up anyway. Happy birthday!'

Pippa's eyes were wide open now, and she bounded down from her cushion to give Paddy a lick. 'It's your birthday!' she woofed. 'I don't mind being woken up for that!' Pippa fluttered her yellow wings and clapped her paws together. 'Happy birthday, Paddy!'

Paddy grinned. He wasn't in
trouble after all! He glanced up
at the strange shape again. 'So
. . . *is* that my present?' he panted
eagerly.

His mum laughed. 'No, it
isn't. It's a bluebird's nest! And
it's a good job you didn't manage
to climb up there, because it's full
of eggs that are almost ready to
hatch. Now, why don't you have
some birthday breakfast?'

25

While their mum prepared some poppy-seed bread with home-made blackberry jam, Pippa and Paddy fetched their wooden plates. They scrambled up on to their toadstools, and soon they were tucking in.

'As soon as you've finished, you have to go and do your special job,' Paddy's mum said.

'But it's my birthday!' replied Paddy. 'Can't I just have fun today?'

26

His mum smiled. 'Pollen Puppies *always* have fun, no matter what they're doing.'

'Hmm, yes, that's true,' said Paddy, thumping his tail in agreement.

27

'And you have to go,' said his dad, 'because we need to get your party ready for when you come back.'

'Ooooh!' Paddy's tail began to wag even harder. 'In that case, we'll go right now!'

Paddy and Pippa skipped out of their den into the bright sunshine. They opened their glistening wings and flitted up over the hedges.

It was a beautiful summer's day. Little clouds were drifting across the sky like wisps of candy-floss. Paddy twitched his shiny pink nose and smiled. He could smell the sweet scent of hawthorn blossom and dusky pink roses.

Down below, one of their neighbours, Heidi the Holly Hamster, was nibbling the leaves of a holly bush into shape. She had to start early, so they'd be

ready for Christmas.

'Good morning, Heidi!' Paddy woofed. 'It's my birthday!'

Heidi waved her tiny paw at him. 'I know! Happy birthday, Paddy! See you at your party!'

Paddy and Pippa went on their way. They flew over fairy mushroom rings and a sea of nodding dandelion clocks, then floated down into Honeydew Meadow. The flowers were in full

AAAHHH-TCHOO!

bloom – golden buttercups and purple foxgloves, fiery red poppies and soft, creamy lilies. They looked wonderful, and they were all laden with pollen. All they needed now was a flick from a Pollen Puppy's tail so that new flowers would grow!

When Paddy came in to land, a crowd of puppies gathered round him at once.

'Happy birthday!' they chorused. Then they turned up

32

their noses and gave a happy, doggy howl. 'Wahhoooooooow!'

Paddy wanted to jump for joy.

The puppies set to work, bouncing through the meadow, wagging their tails. Paddy was so excited, his tail batted to and fro in a blur. His mum was right – his special job was fun! And it was more fun than ever on his birthday!

Flick . . . flick . . . flick . . .

Flickflickflick.

Flickety-flickflickflick . . .

Paddy had never wagged his
tail so fast in his life!

And then he heard a noise.

'Aaahhh-tchoo!' sneezed
his friend Petey, one of the other
Pollen Puppies.

'Aaahhh . . . TCHOO!' sneezed
Polly, a pretty puppy with silky
grey ears.

'AAAHHH . . . TCHOO!

AAAHHH . . . TCHOO!
AAAHHH . . . TCHOO!'

Paddy looked around the meadow. His tail had flicked up clouds and clouds of pollen. The other Pollen Puppies had all stopped. Their sparkly wings were flat. Pippa was wiping her eyes with her paws. Others were spluttering and sneezing. Some were rubbing their button noses, trying to stop them from tickling.

35

'Paddy!' cried Petey. 'You're working so fast that you've flicked ten times too much pollen! Aaahhh . . . tchoo!'

'Ooowww!' howled Paddy in dismay. He looked back at his furry tail, which was still waving to and fro. 'What do you think I should do?'

'We know you're excited about your birthday,' a spotty puppy called Pepper said. 'So maybe

you should use up some of your energy. Why don't you go to flick pollen in Golden Meadow? Maybe by the time you've flown all the way there, your tail won't be wagging so hard.'

'Oh, yes,' woofed Paddy. He shook his wings and did a little jig. 'That's a great idea! Look out, Golden Meadow – the Birthday Pollen Puppy is coming your way!'

CHAPTER THREE

Happy Birthday to Me!

Paddy launched himself into the air. He waved goodbye to his friends in Honeydew Meadow and set off through the Heart of

Misty Wood. It was lovely and cool among the trees. Paddy swooped around the towering tree-trunks, practising his flying skills.

'Happy birthday to me, happy birthday to meeeee!' he sang.

He zoomed up high to wag his tail at a woodpecker, who was peck-peck-pecking up in a tree. Then he flitted down to do a somersault over a rotting log.

He had just started humming

his birthday tune again when he
spotted a lovely big pile of leaves
sitting under a beech tree. They
looked *so* inviting! Paddy flew
higher and hovered for a moment.
'This will be fun!' he giggled to
himself.

He pointed his shiny pink nose
at the pile and began diving down.
His wings whirred as they got
faster and faster and faster . . .

'Happy birthday, dear Paddy!'

he warbled at the top of his voice as he skidded into the leaves at top speed. 'Happy birthday to MEEEEEE!'

The leaves flew everywhere. Paddy rolled around in them, kicking his paws wildly. There were brown leaves, red leaves, yellow leaves, gold leaves. There were big leaves, small leaves, fat leaves, thin leaves.

'Oh, this is so much fun.

43

I'm having the best birthday ever!'
Paddy exclaimed as he flicked the
leaves with his tail.

But then, suddenly, he heard a
voice.

'HEY!'

Paddy jumped.

'HEY!' the voice called again,
sounding very cross.

Paddy looked around.

'Yes, YOU!'

Paddy brushed the leaves
from his fur with his paws. Then
he plucked one leaf from between
his wings. 'Who is it?' he squeaked,

feeling a teeny bit scared.

'It's Hattie the Hedgerow Hedgehog,' said the voice. 'And you've just spoiled my hard work!'

Oh dear.

Oh dear, oh dear, oh dear!

All at once, Paddy understood why there had been such a big pile of leaves sitting in the middle of the wood. The Hedgerow Hedgehogs had their own special job, just like all the other fairy

animals in Misty Wood. They used their prickles to pick up leaves and keep the wood tidy. Paddy clapped his paw to his mouth as Hattie fluttered out from behind the beech tree.

'I'm sorry,' Paddy whimpered. 'I didn't think the pile belonged to anyone.'

Hattie landed on the ground in front of Paddy. Her prickles were fluffed out in all directions,

so she looked like a big spiky ball.

She sighed. 'What's your name,

little Pollen Puppy?'

'I'm Paddy. And I'm really,
truly sorry,' whispered Paddy.
He bent his head so that his ears
drooped over his eyes. He even
managed to stop his tail wagging,
just to show how sorry he was.

'It took me all morning to
get those cleared up,' Hattie said,
looking sadly at the leaves. 'And
when I saw you messing them up
– and singing a song while you
did it – I thought you were ruining

my work on purpose.' She rustled
her rusty-brown wings and sniffed.
'But you do look *very* sorry, I must
say. What was that song you were
singing?'

'Happy birthday,' Paddy
mumbled, 'to – to me.'

Hattie folded away her wings.
'To you, eh?'

Paddy nodded his silky head.
'Yes. You see, I was so excited
about my birthday, and when

50

I saw your leaves I just thought they would be wonderful to play in,' he explained. 'I didn't mean to ruin anything, I really didn't. In fact, I'm on my way to do my own special job. Even though it's my birthday.'

'I see.' Hattie rubbed her chin with her delicate black paw. Then she sighed. 'Well, never mind. There aren't too many leaves at this time of year. I don't suppose it

51

will take me long to tidy them up.'

'Oh, but I can help you!'

Paddy barked. He allowed his

tail to give a little wag. 'I have

so much energy because it's my

birthday, I have to use some of it

up before I get to Golden Meadow.

Otherwise I'll flick too much pollen

and make all the other Pollen

Puppies sneeze again!'

Hattie looked surprised.

'That's nice of you.' She smiled.

'And it would be fun to have someone to tidy with. I'm all on my own in this part of the wood.'

'Really?' said Paddy. 'Come on then, let's get started.'

Paddy watched as Hattie fluffed out her prickles. Then she curled herself into a ball, and rolled along the ground so that her prickles picked up the leaves. She looked so funny covered in leaves that Paddy started to laugh.

53

'You look more like a *hedge* than a hedgehog!' he giggled.

Hattie grinned. 'That's how I'm supposed to look!' she told him, shaking the leaves into a pile. 'Come on now. You try!'

Paddy rolled through the

leaves, then peered round to look at his back. It hadn't worked. Not a single leaf had stuck to his soft fur.

'Oh, dear,' he said. 'I suppose I'll have to find another way to help you.'

'Try collecting them in your mouth instead,' Hattie suggested.

So Paddy scampered off and picked up a mouthful of leaves. They felt so tickly against his tongue he had to try really hard not to laugh. He dropped the leaves on top of Hattie's and then he went back for some more. He couldn't collect as many leaves in his mouth as Hattie could with her prickles, so he had to run to and

fro, to and fro, his ears and wings
flapping. It was hard work! But, at
last, all of the leaves were in a neat
pile again.

Hattie wiped her forehead
with her paw. 'Phew,' she said.

'We did it. Thank you, Paddy!'

'That's all right,' grinned Paddy. 'Now, I really must be getting to Golden Meadow. But you'll come to my birthday party later, won't you? It's at the Hawthorn Hedgerows.'

'I'd love to!' said Hattie. 'How exciting – a new friend and a birthday party, all in one day!'

CHAPTER FOUR

Where's My Breakfast?

With a last wave to Hattie, Paddy
flew off through the Heart of Misty
Wood and out into the open lands
beyond. Soon, he was soaring over

Dewdrop Spring, where the Cobweb Kittens collected their dewdrops in the morning.

The water was twinkling in the sun. It looked so magical that Paddy couldn't resist fluttering towards the surface to trail his paws in the cool, clear water. Blue and pink dragonflies skimmed along beside him, while bright green frogs hopped jauntily across the lily pads. Then Paddy spotted

something else. Something that

made him think about his party.

On the bank of the lake, next to an

old, gnarled log, sat a little pile

of acorns.

61

'Acorns!' Paddy cried. 'The best birthday parties *always* have acorns!'

He flew down and landed next to them. They were the biggest, roundest acorns he'd ever seen. He tried to remember the very best games you could play with acorns. He loved *Hide the Acorn*, but he couldn't play that on his own. There was *Pass the Acorn*, but that needed friends too. Then he

remembered how one of the Bud Bunnies had once shown him how to juggle. He imagined showing off to all his friends as they arrived at his party, juggling acorns high in the air.

'Up in the air, up in the air, juggle the acorns, if you dare!' he chanted.

Paddy grabbed a handful of acorns and began to throw them from one paw to another.

But it was a lot harder to catch them than he remembered. One of the acorns flew up much too high. When it came down again it landed in Dewdrop Spring with a big *PLOP*!

'Oh, dear,' murmured Paddy. 'Never mind. There are still plenty of acorns left.'

He threw them up again.

'One, two, three, four, I'll catch them with my tail and my

nifty paw!'

Paddy leaped about, trying to catch the acorns. But as they came down, his paws got all tangled. *Thud! Bump!* went two of the acorns, landing on the bank and rolling into the water with a *plop*. As Paddy chased after them, a third acorn flew over his head and landed in the pond with a tinkly *splish*.

Then he heard a voice.

'Where's my breakfast?'

Paddy spun round. There, sitting on the log, was a Stardust Squirrel. Usually, Paddy would have been very happy. He loved Stardust Squirrels. Their fur glistened silver or dusky red, and they had delicate wings to match. When they shook their bushy tails they sent showers of stardust all over Misty Wood. But this one wasn't shaking his tail. Instead, he

was looking a bit cross.

'B-b-b-breakfast?' stuttered
Paddy.

'Yes.' The squirrel nodded his
silvery head. 'I put a perfect pile of
delicious acorns right next to this
log. And now they've all gone!'

'Oh, dear,' said Paddy,
hanging his head in shame.

The squirrel looked at Paddy,
with his head to one side. 'I don't
suppose you might know what

happened to them?'

Paddy laid his wings flat along his back and tucked his tail between his legs. He felt terrible.

'I'm so sorry,' he said sadly. 'I didn't know they were your breakfast. It's my birthday, you see, and I'm so excited – I just thought I'd see if I could juggle them. I thought it might be a fun trick for my party, but . . .' He looked sadly towards the lake.

The Stardust Squirrel
raised his tufty ears in disbelief.
'You were trying to juggle?' he
squeaked. 'I've never seen a Pollen
Puppy juggle.'

'No, well, it's not what we do
best,' admitted Paddy.

'And what *do* you do best?'

Paddy cocked his head to one
side. 'Wag our tails.'

'That's what I thought,' said
the Stardust Squirrel. Then he put

his paws to his mouth and started
to shake.

Paddy stared. The squirrel
was wobbling all over. Even his
bushy tail had joined in. It was
sending clouds of stardust into
the air, covering everything with
glitter.

Then Paddy realised what
was happening. The squirrel was
laughing!

'Haw haw haw haw!' the

squirrel roared. 'A Pollen Puppy who thinks he can juggle! I never heard anything so funny in the whole of Misty Wood!' Then he stopped suddenly. 'I'm sorry. I don't mean to laugh at you –

especially on your birthday. It's just that . . . that . . .'

He tried to make his face serious, but he couldn't quite manage it. His nose and whiskers twitched, and his silver wings began to wiggle.

Paddy thought of how all the acorns had plopped into the lake. It must have looked very funny. He began to giggle too. Soon they were both laughing so hard that

they rolled around together on
the bank of the lake, jiggling their
wings and clutching their sides.

At last, they sat up and wiped
their eyes. The Stardust Squirrel
had covered the whole bank with
stardust.

'Thank you, Pollen Puppy,'
he said. 'You might have lost my
breakfast, but you've made me
laugh. What's your name?'

'Paddy. What's yours?'

'I'm Sammy,' replied the squirrel. 'Now, I suppose I'd better go and find some more acorns.'

'Oh, no,' said Paddy, wagging his tail. 'I should find them for you.' He pointed back towards the Heart of Misty Wood. 'There are lots of big oak trees just over there. Come on, I'll show you.'

Together, they flexed their wings and flew off towards the giant oak trees. When they got

75

there, Paddy leaped and bounced around, sniffing out the plumpest, ripest acorns. Soon, Sammy had an even bigger pile than before!

'Thank you, Paddy!' said Sammy. 'Looks like I've found a new friend as well as breakfast!'

'You're welcome,' Paddy woofed. 'Now, I'd better go and do my work in Golden Meadow. But will you come to my party later, at Hawthorn Hedgerows?'

Sammy twitched his bushy

tail, sprinkling stardust all over his

acorns. 'Oh, yes please!' he cried.

'That would be great fun!'

CHAPTER FIVE

Paddy's Perfect Cushion

As Sammy started munching his breakfast, Paddy took off again for Golden Meadow, waving goodbye as he went. But his yellow

wings began to feel heavy.

Flap . . . flaaap . . . flaaaap . . .

Paddy was flying slower
and slower. He'd woken up very
early and it had been such a busy
morning. Now he felt so tired that
he was starting to sink towards
the ground. 'How will I ever reach
Golden Meadow?' he yelped to
himself.

Just below him, he saw a
pretty hill covered in nodding

buttercups. And right on top of the hill sat a cushion. It was made of the softest, comfiest moss Paddy had ever seen, and it reminded him of his own snuggly bed.

Ooh, he thought. *That looks perfect for a nap. Just a quick nap . . .*

He floated down and flopped on to the cushion. He laid his head on the moss and closed his eyes. He was so tired that he fell asleep at once. And soon, he was dreaming.

PADDY'S PERFECT CUSHION

It was a beautiful dream. He was at the most wonderful birthday party in the world, and he was surrounded by presents. Everyone was cheering and clapping. The trees were decorated with daisy chains, and the air fizzed with stardust. Birds were twittering up in the branches, and all the fairy animals were singing birthday songs. Best of all, his mum and dad had given him the

most juicy, tasty bone he'd ever
seen. Paddy was dancing round it,
wiggling his body and waggling
his tail. Then all his Pollen Puppy
friends linked paws with him and
joined in.

But something wasn't right.

'Oh! What have you done?' he
heard a squeaky voice say.

Paddy frowned. He tried to
grab his lovely bone, but when
his little jaws snapped shut, it

disappeared! Paddy began to panic. He couldn't possibly lose his birthday bone . . .

'I said, what have you DONE?' the voice squeaked again, louder this time.

Paddy jumped. His eyes popped open. And there, tapping him on the nose with a little paw, was a Moss Mouse. He had pure white fur, the finest blue and white wings . . . and a big frown

84

on his tiny face.

'Oh!' yelped Paddy as he remembered where he was. 'I was dreaming about a bone. A beautiful, juicy bone . . .' He rubbed his eyes sadly.

'I know,' sniffed the Moss Mouse.

'You know? How?' Paddy cocked his ears in surprise.

'Look what you've done to my cushion!' The Moss Mouse

started hopping up and down. 'I'm Magnifico the Moss Mouse and I pride myself on my moss cushions. This one was as round and smooth as a springtime moon. *Now* see what shape it is!'

Paddy jumped off the cushion. He stared. The mouse was right. It wasn't round any more. The cushion was shaped like a huge bone!

'My tail must have wagged it into that shape while I was

dreaming,' Paddy said, still staring
at the cushion in disbelief.

'Yes!' exclaimed Magnifico,
folding his front paws. 'That's
exactly what it did.'

Paddy felt very upset. His over-excited tail was causing all sorts of problems today. Moss Mice worked so hard to make all the lovely moss cushions in Misty Wood. They got up at dawn to hunt out the fluffiest moss from the shadiest valleys and the deepest dells. Then they spent hours patting it into shape.

'I'm really sorry,' Paddy said. 'It's my birthday, you see, and I'm

all excited. It wasn't just any old bone that I was dreaming about. It was a *birthday* bone.'

'Oh!' said Magnifico, twitching his tiny pink nose. 'Well, that does make a difference.'

'Does it?' Paddy pricked his ears hopefully. 'You mean you're not cross any more? I'll help you get the cushion back into its proper shape, I promise!'

'Hmm. Well, let's see.'

Magnifico walked all round the
cushion. He looked at it one way.
Then he looked at it another way.
With a blurry buzz of his blue
and white wings, he clambered up
on to it. He ran to one end of the
cushion and peered off the edge.
Then he scampered to the other
end and peered off that side too.
Paddy watched him, holding his
breath.

At last, Magnifico bounced

back over to sit in front of Paddy
and began to chuckle.

'I think it's perfect,' he said.

'Perfect?' Paddy wasn't sure
he'd heard correctly.

'I've never had a cushion in
the shape of a bone before,' said
Magnifico. 'Especially not in the
shape of a *birthday* bone. I'm
going to keep it, just as it is – in
your honour!'

'Oooooh!' exclaimed Paddy.

'Thank you! Will it stay here for a
long time?'

'Of course,' said Magnifico.
He smoothed back his whiskers
proudly. 'I told you. I only make

the very best quality cushions.'

'So, I can come here and sit on it any time I like?' Paddy panted.

'I don't see why not,' said Magnifico. 'What's your name?'

'I'm Paddy.'

'We can name it, if you like.' Magnifico paused for a second. 'How about, *Paddy's Birthday Bone Cushion*?'

'Oh, yes, yes, yes!' Paddy

yapped. 'Thank you!' He jumped
up and padded the cushion with
his paws. He'd come and have a
nap here as often as he could. He
opened his wings and flapped back
down to sit next to Magnifico.
'In return, please will you come
to my birthday party later? It's at
the Hawthorn Hedgerows.'

Magnifico's shiny eyes lit up.
'You're having a party?'

Paddy nodded.

94

'A real one, not a dream one?'

'Yes.' Paddy's tail began wagging wildly.

'Wonderful,' sighed Magnifico. 'I love parties.'

'This one's going to be the best in the world,' Paddy told him. 'Even better than the one in my dream!' He glanced up and saw that the sun was now high in the sky. 'Ooh, I'd better go, or I'll never get all my work done in

Golden Meadow. See you later,
Magnifico – and thank you again
for my birthday cushion!'

CHAPTER SIX

The Best Birthday Party Ever

Hovering over Golden Meadow
at last, Paddy was bursting with
happiness. The meadow's rainbow
colours shimmered in the sunshine,

and he could just see the tips of other puppies' tails as they wagged their way around the swaying flower stems.

Paddy swooped down and landed softly. He was still excited, but he was careful to keep his tail much calmer now. *Flick . . . flick . . . flick . . .* it went. Pollen rose lightly and floated off on the gentle breeze, while other flowers opened their petals to welcome it to a new home.

When half the dandelion
clocks had blown their seeds away,
Paddy knew that it was time to
go home. He had spread *lots* of
pollen! He rose into the air and
fluttered back towards Hawthorn
Hedgerows.

What an amazing day I've had!
he thought. He'd made three new
friends – Hattie, Sammy and
Magnifico. He'd helped them tidy
leaves and collect acorns. He'd

99

flicked more pollen than he'd
ever thought a Pollen Puppy
could. And he hadn't even had
his birthday party yet! If only he
didn't feel quite so tired . . .

As he floated down towards
the hedgerows, Paddy's eyelids
began to droop. He thought
longingly of his little moss bed.
Maybe he could have a snooze
before all the fun began.

But then, just as he landed

next to a purple toadstool, he
heard a shout. A BIG shout.

'SURPRISE!'

Paddy peeped over the
toadstool. Just ahead, in the
clearing next to the hawthorn
bushes, his whole family was
waving and cheering. Pippa was
bouncing up and down. And they
weren't alone. All the other Pollen
Puppies were there, and all his
friends from across Misty Wood.

There were Cobweb Kittens and Holly Hamsters and Bud Bunnies and even a couple of Moonbeam Moles – and everyone knew that moles preferred to go out in the dark.

Then he heard a rustle of rusty-brown wings.

Hattie the Hedgerow Hedge-hog was there!

Next, he saw a bushy silver tail, sprinkling stardust everywhere.

102

Sammy the Stardust Squirrel was there!

Then he heard a cheeky squeak at his feet. He looked down.

Magnifico the Moss Mouse was there!

'Happy Birthday, Paddy!' everyone cried.

The glade had been decorated just as Paddy had imagined in his dream – only it was even prettier!

The cobwebs shimmered with extra dewdrops, while garlands of bluebells and poppies adorned all the bushes.

The air filled with the sound of fluttering fairy wings as Paddy's friends came forward with presents. Even his new friends had brought something! Hattie had brought a bowl made of sycamore leaves. Magnifico had brought a miniature moss cushion. And

as for Sammy – first he filled the glade with shimmering stardust. Then, from behind his back, he brought out a whole parcel of conkers and acorns to play with!

'Time for games, everyone!' cried Paddy's dad.

Soon everyone had joined hands and they all danced in a circle, singing *Ring-a-ring-an-Acorn* at the tops of their voices. Then they played *Conker Catch*, before

spreading out to play *Hide the Acorn*.

Paddy had never had so much fun!

At last, happy and weary,

they gathered for the birthday

picnic. Paddy's mum had spread

out a big mat of pearly reeds

from Moonshine Pond, and it was

laden with treats. Paddy's eyes nearly popped out when he saw everything! There were cowslip tarts, daisy pies, fairy fancies and buttercup buns, along with more honeysuckle fizz and elderflower pop than even Paddy could dream of.

But before they began to tuck in, Paddy's dad came bounding out of their den with something else. Paddy's tail began to wag.

Would it be . . . ?

Could it be . . . ?

Paddy yelped happily as his dad handed him a gift wrapped in silvery leaves. As Paddy began to pull at it with his teeth, he was so excited that his whole body started to tremble.

Would it be . . . ?

Could it be . . . ?

One corner of the wrapping came open. Paddy sniffed with his pink button nose.

It *smelled* like a bone.

He tore some more of the leaves away.

It *looked* like a bone.

The last piece of wrapping dropped off, and Paddy bounced up and down with joy.

111

It WAS a bone!

And it was even more juicy and tasty than the one he'd seen in his dream.

'Thank you, thank you!' he barked, jumping round in circles.

Everyone clapped and cheered, then they began to eat and drink. Paddy gave his bone one lick, then decided to save it for later. There was so much delicious party food, he wanted to try it all. As he slurped honeysuckle fizz and chomped a daisy pie he decided that this really was the best birthday party ever!

In the distance, the sun was dipping towards Sundown Hill.

Golden rays played with the stardust in the air, while the shadows in the clearing grew longer.

Paddy thought there couldn't possibly be any more treats. He'd had so many! But his mum and dad had disappeared again, and all the fairy guests began to whisper behind their paws. Where had they gone? What were they up to?

Suddenly, there was a flurry of fur at the entrance to the family den. Paddy turned to look, and saw his mum, dad and sister Pippa holding a birthday cake between them. It was made of hazelnuts and rosehips, and it had a garland of ivy leaves tied in a bow around it. On the top, waving gently, were birthday dandelion clocks for Paddy to blow.

Everyone cheered again, and

burst into song.

'Happy birthday, dear Paddy! Happy birthday to you!' they chorused.

'Happy birthday, dear Paddy! Happy birthday to meeeee!' Paddy sang along. His tail was wagging so fast, it nearly blew all the seeds from the dandelion clocks!

Just as the song came to an end, Paddy heard something else.

Something tuneful and tinkly. It was coming from their den . . .

Cheep!

Cheep cheep!

Cheep cheep cheep!

Paddy cocked his ears. 'What was that?' he asked.

His mum smiled. 'It's the bluebird chicks!' she told him. 'They've just hatched. There are three of them – come and look!'

With a last burst of energy,

Paddy bounded over to the nest.
And there they were – three tiny
balls of fluff with a teeny beak
each, begging for food. And
to think they'd hatched on his
birthday . . .

'They're the best present of
all!' Paddy cried.

'Well, we're all happy that
you've had such a lovely day,'
smiled his mum. 'But don't forget
to blow your birthday clocks!'

THE BEST BIRTHDAY PARTY EVER

The birthday cake was sitting in the middle of the picnic. Paddy rushed back. As he filled his cheeks with air, he thought he was the luckiest Pollen Puppy in the whole of Misty Wood.

'One, two, three, *blow*!' chanted the crowd.

Paddy blew. The dandelion seeds flew up in a cloud, then floated off. Some of the guests laughed and chased after them.

But not Paddy.

Paddy had finally run out of puff.

He lay down on his soft, mossy cushion and, with a happy sigh, he fell fast asleep.

Misty Wood word search

Can you find all these words from
the story in this fun word search?

PUPPY
TAIL
PARTY
PRESENT
BONE
WAG
ACORN
DREAM
FLICK
GAME

```
E A C O R N O E O H R V M I S
B E H V S G A M E N N Y F N N
O P F H N I E H P S E T D O R
N E D I S T T A R R E S D A E
E P I S O H H E E S P O D E I
D R W A G S L Y S T N A R S T
R L A H S P I C E S D Y U T E
E U E P S F M I N A O D A S D
A U A S Y C L S T A S A E O E
M F I P R P E I R I S L L N T
S O M E N S U P C R R F S T A
I Y O R W G R P A K E E N S I
F E M H L I H F P R C H E T L
N R T P A C E E V Y T I U N O
B K T A O Q D T C T W Y T S T
```

All about YOUR birthday!

When is your birthday?

....

How old will you be on your next birthday?

....

What present would you like?

....

What would you most like to do?

....

Which people would you like to be there?

....

A very happy birthday!

Paddy gets VERY excited about his birthday. What are your three favourite things about birthdays?

1. ....
2. ....
3. ....

What other special occasions are really exciting?

1. ....
2. ....
3. ....

Join the dots

Follow the numbers and join up all
the dots to make a lovely picture.
Start with dot number 1.

Can you guess what Paddy is holding?

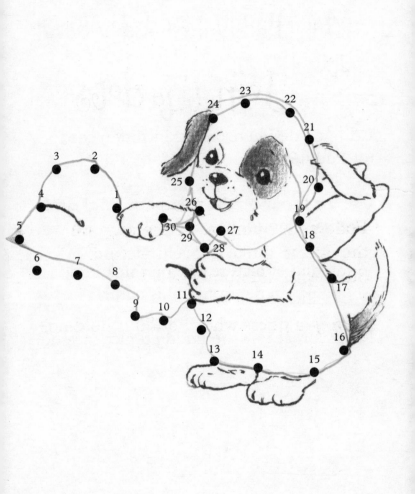

Make Paddy a birthday card!

Can you design a special birthday card for Paddy?

Use the frame on the next page. Make the card as colourful as you can!

What kind of picture do you think Paddy would like on the front of his card?

Don't forget to write Paddy a nice message!

Fairy Animals
of Misty Wood

Look out for
Betsy the Bunny
and lots more
coming soon . . .

Meet the

Fairy Animals
of Misty Wood

There's a whole world to explore!

Download the FREE *Fairy Animals*
app and visit **fairyanimals.com** for lots
of gorgeous goodies . . .

✳ Free stuff
✳ Games
✳ Write to your favourite characters
✳ Step inside Misty Wood
✳ Send us your cute pet pictures
✳ Make your own fairy wings!

Available on the
App Store